A Big Guy
Took My Ball!

By **Mo Willems**

By **Mo Willems**

An **ELEPHANT & PIGGIE** Book

Pigs Make
Me Sneeze!

By **Mo Willems**

An **ELEPHANT & PIGGIE** Book

My New
Friend Is So
Fun!

By **Mo Willems**

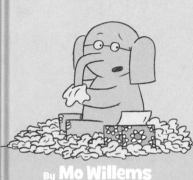

An **ELEPHANT & PIGGIE** Book

A Big Guy
Took My Ball!

By **Mo Willems**

An **ELEPHANT & PIGGIE** Book

My Friend
Is Sad

WITHDRAWN

By **Mo Willems**

An **ELEPHANT & PIGGIE** Book

An **ELEPHANT & PIGGIE** Book

My New
Friend Is So
Fun!

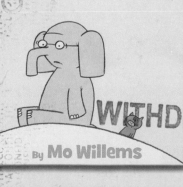

To Greg, Gideon, and the Stampede Team
Biggie Supporters

First Edition, September 2021
10 9 8 7 6 5 4 3 2
FAC-034274-22061
This book is set in Century 725/Monotype; Grilled Cheese/Fontbros; Typography of Coop, Fink, Neutraface/House Industries
Printed in the United States of America
Reinforced binding

Library of Congress Cataloging-in-Publication Control Number: 2020952195
ISBN 978-1-368-07112-3

Visit www.hyperionbooksforchildren.com and www.pigeonpresents.com

# An ELEPHANT & PIGGIE
# BIGGIE!
## Volume 4

# By Mo Willems

Hyperion Books for Children / *New York*

2

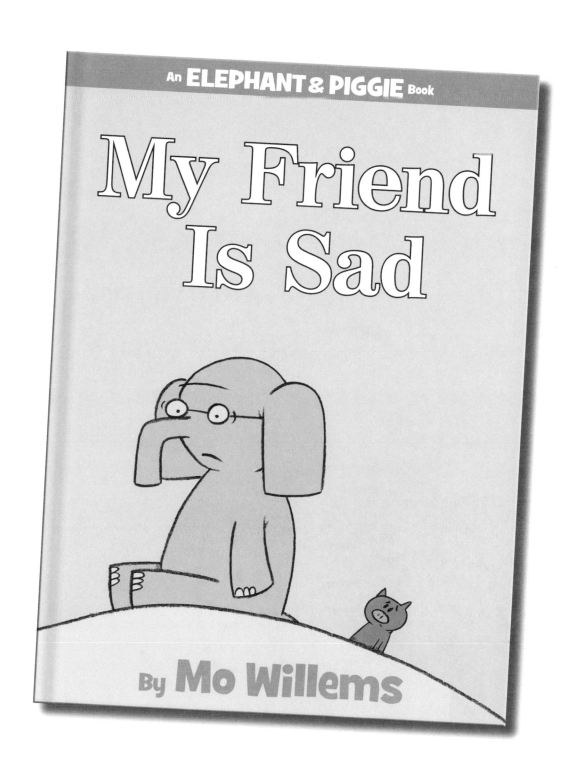

Originally published in April 2007.

# My Friend Is Sad

By **Mo Willems**

An **ELEPHANT & PIGGIE** Book
Hyperion Books for Children / *New York*

Ohhh . . .

A cowboy!

Ohhh . . .

Clowns are funny.
But he is still sad.

26

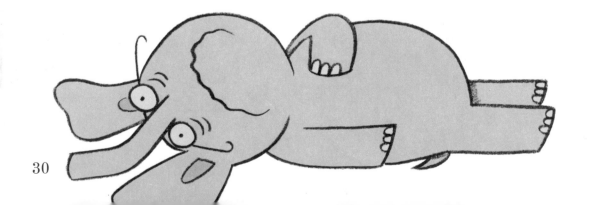

I am sorry. I wanted to make you happy. But you are still sad.

But I was so sad, Piggie.
So very SAD!

But you love cowboys!

41

43

THERE
WAS
MORE!

51

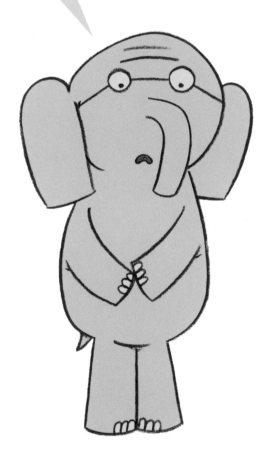

And my best friend
was not there
to see it with me.

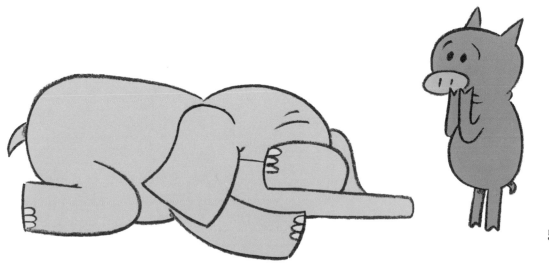

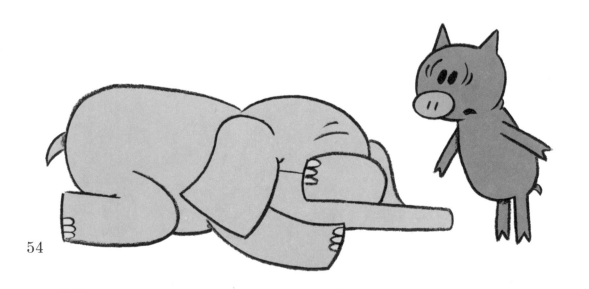

I am here NOW!

My friend is here now!

I need my friends.

You need new glasses....

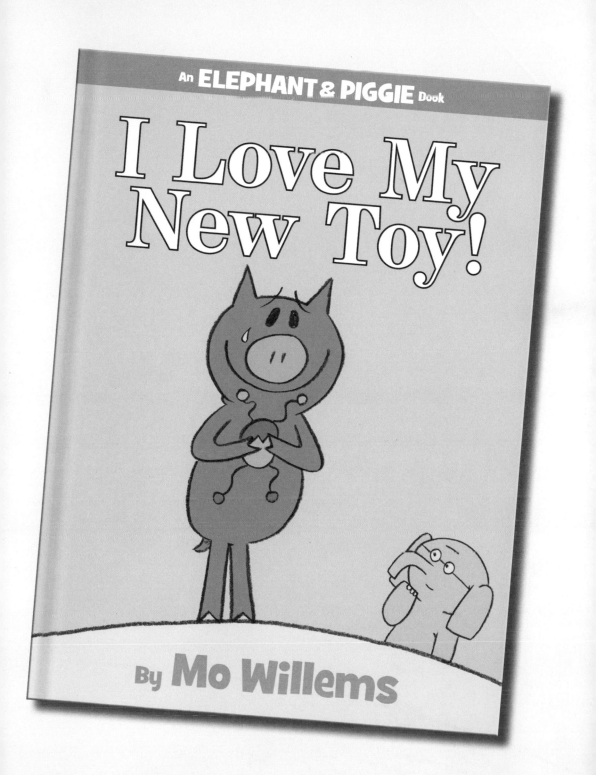

Originally published in June 2008.

# I Love My New Toy!

An **ELEPHANT & PIGGIE** Book

By **Mo Willems**

Hyperion Books for Children / *New York*

Yes!

ZIp!

78

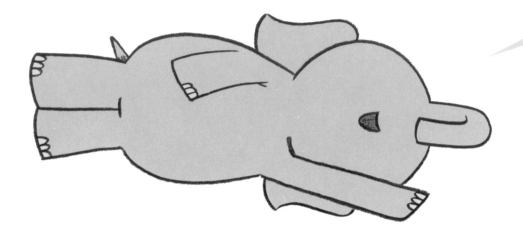

Turn

Here it comes!

ZOOM!

Turn

84

I broke your toy.

You broke my toy.

91

98

My new toy is broken!

AAAAH!

AAAAH!

Cool!

You have a
break-and-snap toy.

SNAP!

Enjoy!

BREAK!

SNAP!

BREAK!

SNAP!

No.

You do not want to play
with my new toy?

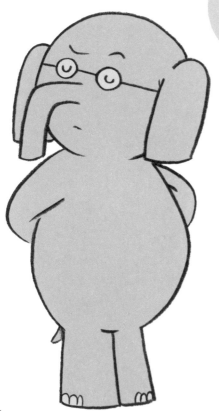

120

Friends are more fun
than toys.

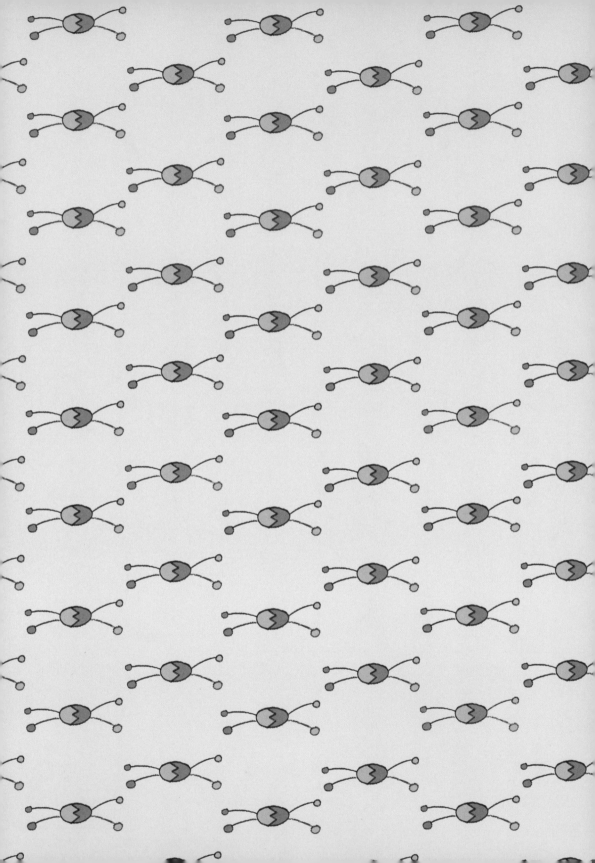

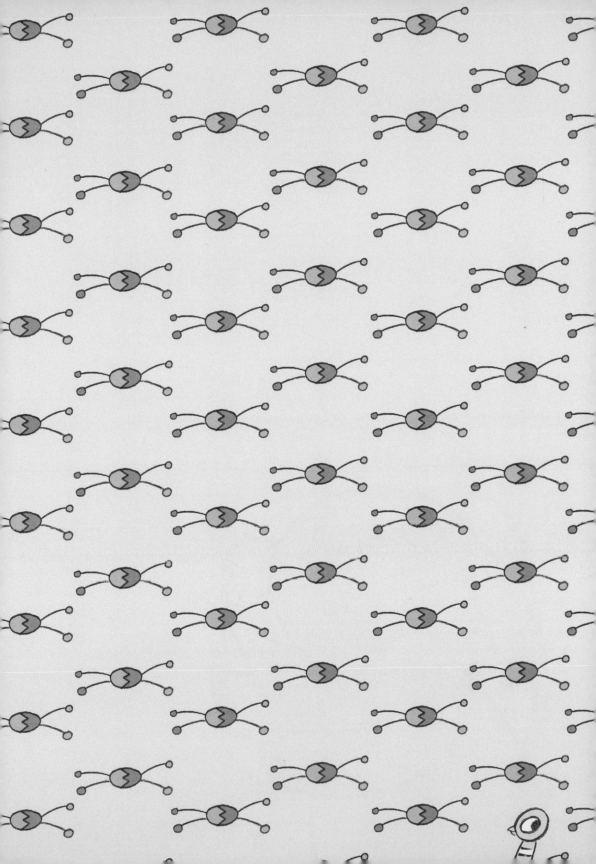

Originally published in October 2009.

# Pigs Make Me Sneeze!

An **ELEPHANT & PIGGIE** Book
By **Mo Willems**

Hyperion Books for Children / *New York*

Gerald!

What do you
want to do
today?

133

135

SNIFF!

141

143

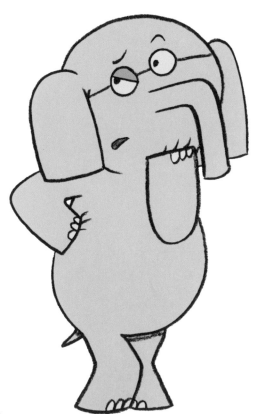

But, if pigs *do* make me sneeze. . . .

153

But, Gerald . . .

158

161

Good-bye.

Gerald . . .

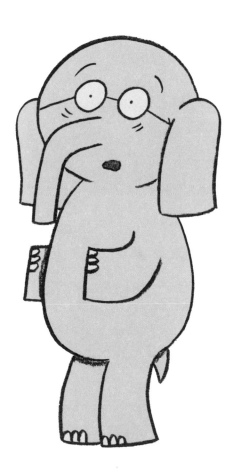

173

THUD!

I do not think cats make you sneeze.

178

Piggie!

Piggie!

184

An **ELEPHANT & PIGGIE** Book

# A Big Guy Took My Ball!

By **Mo Willems**

Originally published in May 2013.

An ELEPHANT & PIGGIE Book

Hyperion Books for Children
New York

By Mo Willems

193

I found a big ball,

197

198

# TOOK
# BALL!

204

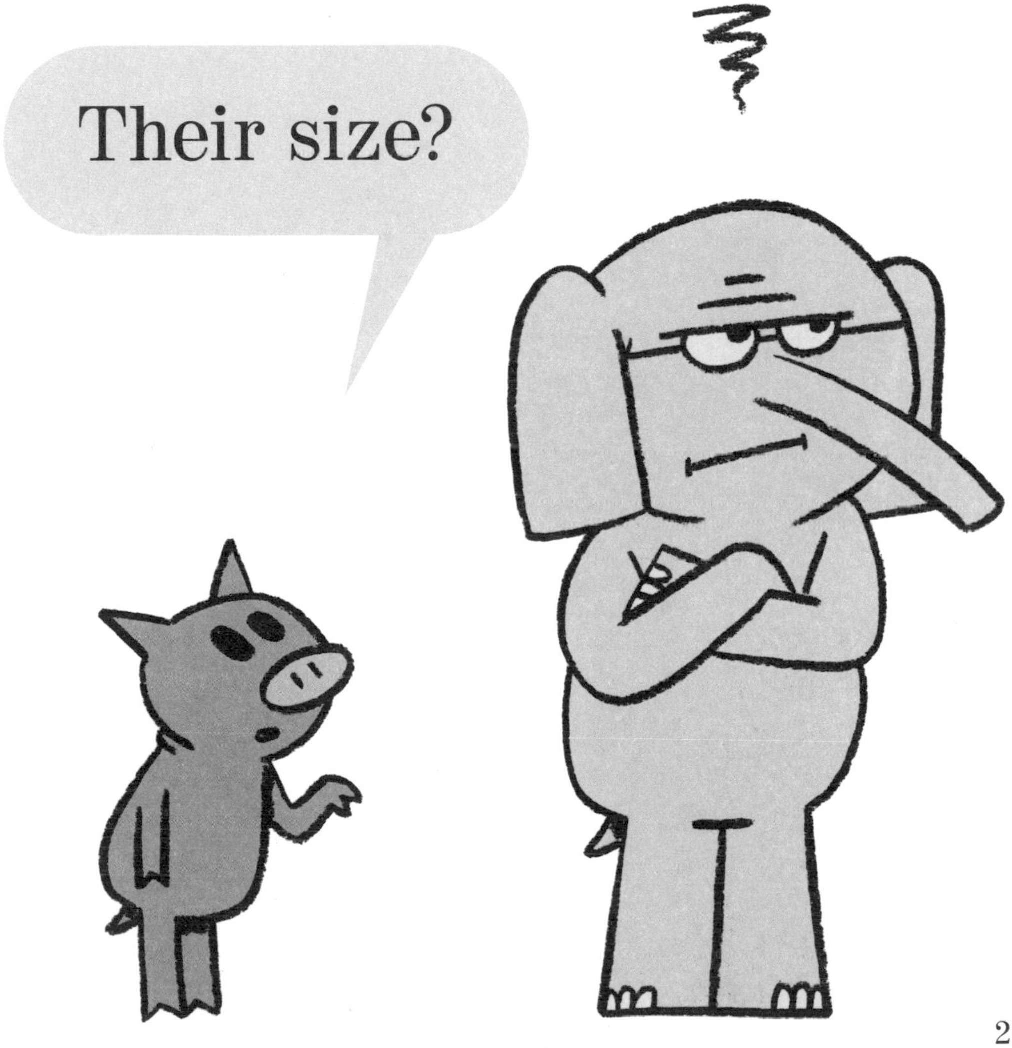
Their size?

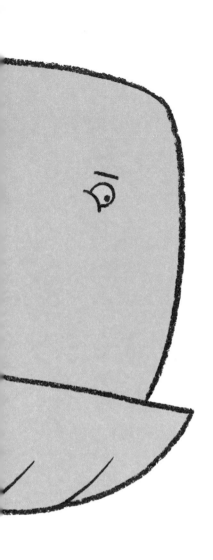

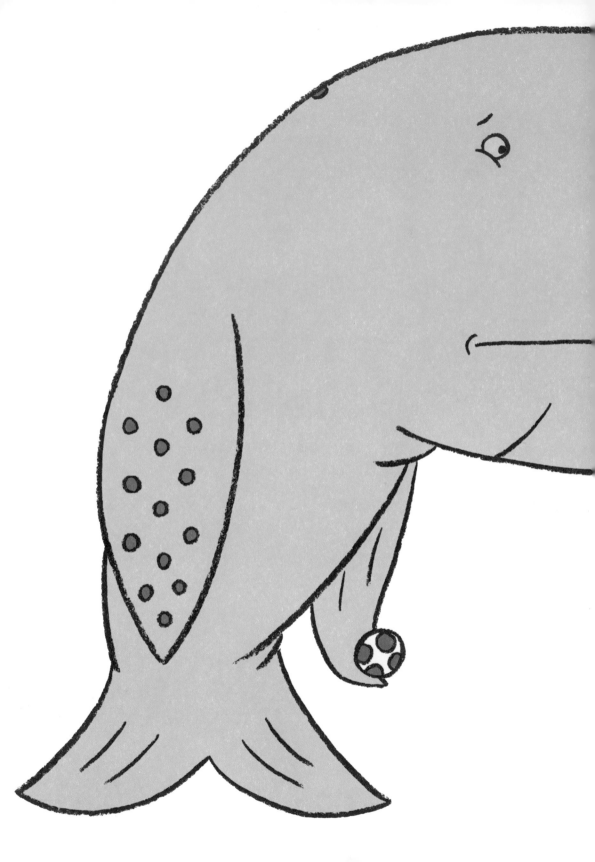

220

He is very **BIG**.

He is bigger than I am.

222

227

# EXCUSE

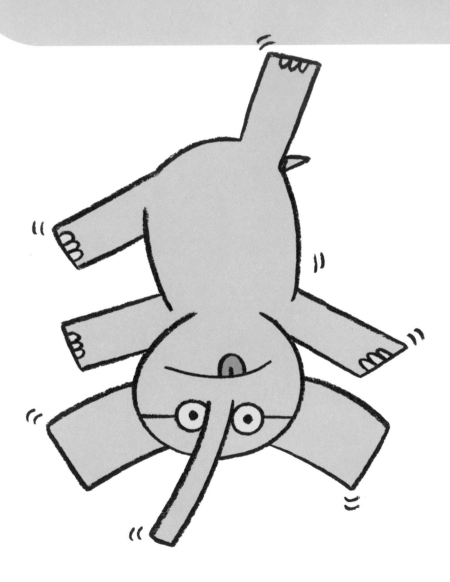

# ME!

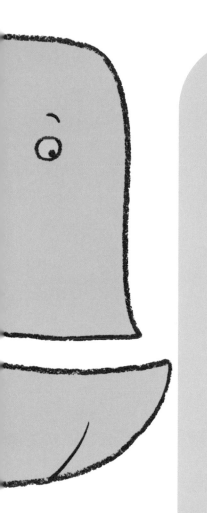

THANK YOU FOR FINDING MY LITTLE BALL.

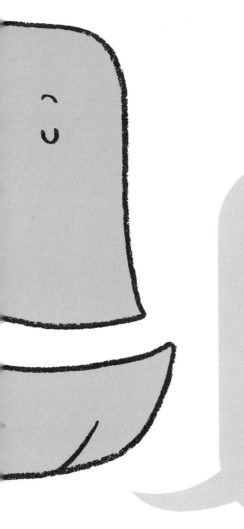

WELL,
I AM
BIG.

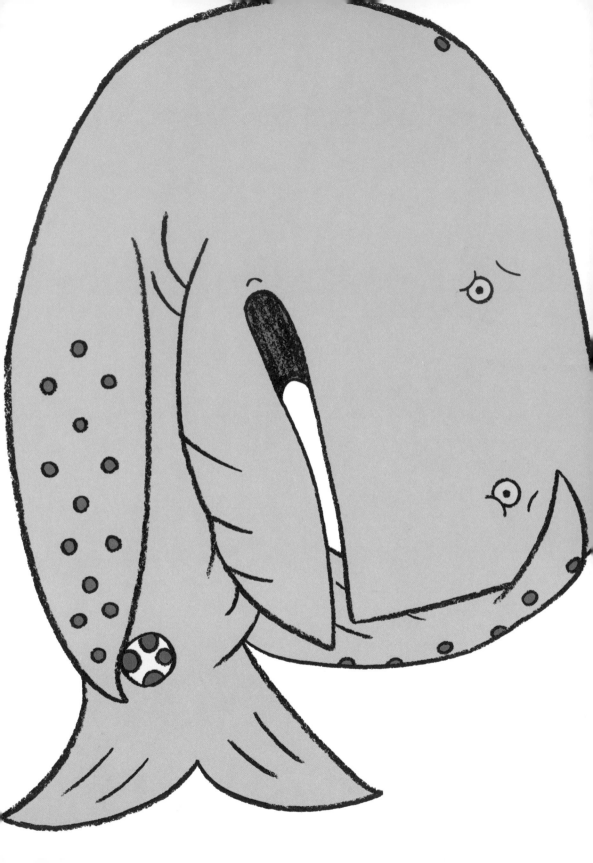

# SO BIG THAT NO ONE WILL PLAY WITH ME.

LITTLE GUYS HAVE
*ALL* THE FUN.

243

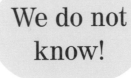

WHAT IS "WHALE BALL"?

We do not know!

We have not made it up yet!

With a *little* help, we can all have

Originally published in June 2014.

An ELEPHANT & PIGGIE Book

Hyperion Books for Children

*New York*

# My New Friend Is So Fun!

By **Mo Willems**

Hi, Gerald!

Piggie just met Brian Bat for the first time.

Now they
are playing.

257

Both Piggie
and Brian
are so nice!

262

265

266

267

274

275

SKID!

SKID!

We have to tell you how much fun we are having!

So much fun!

Best Friend games?

We even made
Best Friend
drawings!

296

Do you want
to see our
drawings?

299

309

# Dear Reader,

# Wow!

You read five Elephant & Piggie adventures in one book! Congratulations!

Elephant and Piggie are best friends. Friendship is not just about having fun. It is also about finding new ways to support someone when they are sad, frustrated, or jealous.

A book can be a friend, too. When I was a kid, my cartoon books made me laugh and helped me think about the world in new ways, just like a friend.

Sometimes friends even make drawings for you. My friend LeUyen Pham drew a cool picture of Elephant and Piggie wearing best-friend clothes. What will Elephant and Piggie be wearing in YOUR drawing of them?

Your pal,

**LeUyen Pham** is a prolific, award-winning author and illustrator. In 2020, she was awarded a Caldecott Honor for her illustrations in *Bear Came Along*. LeUyen wrote and illustrated *The Itchy Book!*, an ELEPHANT & PIGGIE LIKE READING! book. Her other books include *Outside, Inside*; *Big Sister, Little Sister*; and the Princess in Black series, written by Shannon and Dean Hale.

MO WILLEMS'
ELEPHANT & PIGGIE
LIKE READING!

By **Mo Willems**

**An ELEPHANT & PIGGIE Book**

Pigs Make
Me Sneeze!

By **Mo Willems**

**An ELEPHANT & PIGGIE Book**

My New
Friend Is So
Fun!

By **Mo Willems**

**An ELEPHANT & PIGGIE Book**

A Big Guy
Took My Ball!

By **Mo Willems**

My Friend
Is Sad

By **Mo Willems**

**An ELEPHANT & PIGGIE Book**

My New
Friend Is So
Fun!

By **Mo Willems**

**An ELEPHANT & PIGGIE Book**

I Love My
New Toy!